ISBN: 9798362928582

DEDICATION

This one is for all the fans!

-L.

ACKNOWLEDGMENTS

Some of these stories appeared separately in other locations online or offline, at the Storm Crow Manor's vending machine and other illustrious but unusual publishing venues.

CONTENTS

Triceratops and Bottoms

Lola Faust

CHAPTER 1

Erin stood on the balcony of her suite, letting the soft golden rays of sunlight bathe her smooth skin. She was completely nude, her firm breasts thrust out and her perky nipples erect. She closed her eyes and took in a deep breath, craving something deeper…more meaningful.

She opened her eyes and turned around. A draft of cold air brushed over her body and a shiver rushed through her. Just the slight tremor was enough to activate all her nanobots, which drew the silk curtains closed and regulated the temperature in her room, making it warmer. Erin smiled and strutted over to her queen-sized bed.

The thing about the year 2122 was how luxurious everything had become. She had everything she wanted readily available. She didn't even have to snap her fingers like the ancient humans did; all she had to do was think, and her needs would be fulfilled. In theory it was great.. but another thing about having everything you wanted was just how empty and unfulfilling all those things became.

This was the reason Erin decided to pursue her greatest and deepest sexual fantasies. With so much time on her hands, and nanomachines handling practically all work, she had the opportunity to pursue even the craziest reveries.

She settled herself on the warm bed and picked up her 'book of memories'. It was a digital device shaped like a physical book from olden times. It contained multiple exabytes of detailed data from all the wild sexual adventures she'd gone on over the years.

Erin smiled and went through each of the memories.

"I like to think I've done all there is to be done," she mused, tapping her finger on a date. She watched as a hologram played. She was in the middle of a group of bisexual alien races, locked in the most frenetic orgy she'd ever experienced. The blue-skinned alien people were insanely sensual, touching her from all angles; eating her up, making her scream, and fucking her like a slut. She felt her body responding to that memory, sending hot tingles rushing through every nerve of her body.

She'd gone around the various inhabited worlds, having sex with men, women and beings of all races. That was what she chose to do with all her free time. The pleasure always called out to her.

Sometimes she'd simply wake up craving sex and intense orgasms, so much that she'd just pack her bag and head off on a nomadic, hedonistic adventure offworld. Other times she couldn't even wait that long, and would summon a pleasure bot or holographic companion for immediate gratification…

The more she went through these memories, the hornier she got. By the time Erin closed the book her body was heated. She moved her hand over her chest and felt the stiffness of her sensitive nipples; going lower, she felt the hot wetness between her legs, moaning softly as she moved her fingers down there.

She wanted something more; something crazier, and out of this world. The last time she felt this way she went on an adventure to the farthest reaches of the planet and had sex under the splashing colours of the polar lights, and then she'd found herself on a spaceship leaving Earth for the outermost colonies. There, she'd engaged in orgies with a dozen alien races, giving her body to trembling orgasms and explosive pleasures.

Erin raised her fingers and pursed her lips when she saw how wet they were, coated with her sticky juices.

"Gosh, I need a good release," she moaned and fell on her bed, breathing softly. She watched the rhythm of her breasts swelling with each breath; the way her erect nipples poked out. The more she stared at them, the more the craving increased. She rolled off the bed and sauntered into the bathroom.

The doors hissed open as she got close. Adjusting the temperature of the water to a few degrees warmer and increasing the pressure, Erin closed her eyes and let the water do its thing.

I'm starting to find everything oddly erotic, she thought and let out a loud moan when the jets of water hit her most sensitive parts.

She stepped out of the bathroom half an hour later, more frustrated and bored than before. The last time she felt this way she'd travelled to an underground cyborg sex club, barely legal even now, hidden under a dormant volcano in Antarctica, for a series of encounters that had to be struck from the book of memories for fear of legal repercussions…

But what if that was it? What if there wasn't anything better than that?

These fearful thoughts made her uneasy. She lived for the adventure; a lack of it would make life colorless and boring.

Erin decided to play with her new VR cocoon. She'd had it installed in a separate room a month ago, but she'd been too busy to bother testing it. Now seemed to be a perfect time.

She slid into the tight-fitting latex bodysuit and entered the womblike chamber. The lights dimmed all around her and a huge curved screen lit up. It spilt soft lights over her, inviting her in.

Erin put on the headset, fitting it snugly, and placed her hand on the main console. All she had to do was select whatever experience she wanted to have and she'd be immersed into it.

She could be an Old West outlaw, a superhero, a Greek goddess. The possibilities were endless, and it all felt 100% real. *Didn't it?*

"I'll just go for a more intimate option," Erin said to herself.

She entered an open world tailormade to suit her fantasies. It was full of fairies and magical creatures, and she'd oddly decided to add the option of dinosaurs. It was an improvised addition—she'd read something about dinosaurs recently, and it somehow popped up into her mind.

The VR turned out to be an intense affair, almost as good as the real thing. She slid into the Jurassic era and had strangely intense erotic play with different dinosaurs. The simulation was limited, she kept bumping up against artificial barriers, presumably because there were no detailed files from the primeval era. But still… she wondered why it felt…so good. So different from all the others.

She was a sweaty mess by the time she left the virtual world, in need of a burning release.

"If you enjoy this so much, why don't you go for the real thing?" the voice of her apartment said.

"What?"

A small screen came up and a message played out from her resident AI advisor. Erin watched with interest as it talked about a new scientific discovery: the invention of a literal time machine.

CHAPTER 2

The more Erin learnt about the discovery, the more intrigued she became. She had heard rumors of the time machine, of course, but it had seemed only theoretical; not something that was about to become real.

The chronosphere was just what a free spirit like her needed. She quickly secured a pass to the unveiling in a couple of days. It was going to be a great day in the progress of humanity and technology, they promised, with applications in any number of industrial and medical fields.

"You had me at time travel," Erin said

to herself, barely able to contain her excitement.

A couple of days later, Erin found herself at the unveiling of the new machine. Presentations were made on wide holoscreens; lights dimmed all around, immersing them into the images splashing on the screens as the man on the podium posed questions and dazzled the audience—including a wide-eyed Erin.

"Imagine what it would be like, being able to go back in time and relive moments you never would have been able to dream of. Time is like a massive thread interwoven across infinite realities. It's been a long time coming, but we did it."

A deafening round of applause echoed throughout the air. Erin was thrilled by the idea of going back in time. The present was somewhat boring at this point. She'd done everything there was to do; travelled all around, so it only made sense that the next step would be journeying to the past.

She raised her hand and drew the attention of the speaker. He pointed at her and she beamed, feeling like a nerdy girl at her convention.

"How far back in time can we travel?" she asked, and people around her nodded and mumbled; she'd read their thoughts.

"That's a great question," the speaker said. He went ahead to show a simulation of what it would be like to travel back to the past.

"The simple answer is this: you cannot travel beyond any time period more recent than the Jurassic era."

Murmurs washed through the crowd. Erin listened carefully, already picturing the wild Jurassic, a little scepticism trickling in. *What sort of adventure could one embark on during such ancient times?* She wondered. She'd hoped to travel back in time to a crazy era, maybe have sex in the deep trenches of the WW1 combatants. Dangerous, sure, but it would be worth it.

Besides, she would be safe because she had all her gadgets to protect her: forcefields, rebreathers, cloaking devices.

Her mind snapped back to the moment as the speaker explained further.

"It is just for the fear of damaging human timelines. Time, remember, is like a thread. Snip the wrong end and it unravels hundreds of thousands of events, most of which would lead to the complete erasure of many of us."

The speaker paused for a second, holding their attention. "Imagine someone making a silly mistake and wiping off the timeline that would lead to the invention of time travel. It would be terrible!"

After the presentation, chances were given to volunteers to try out the invention. A lot of people were afraid because of the Jurassic era and the danger it posed; while others felt it would be safe to have other people have a go at it until all faults were ironed out.

Not Erin. She jumped at the chance as soon as it was offered, ready to time travel to the past and see what adventures she could have.

She was taken to a room where she was fitted with protective devices—force fields and rebreathers and other useful items—and of course, her time travel belt fully charged and ready to go.

She was a little restless with excitement as they went through the procedure with her, and enlightened her on the safety measures and what to do when the charge became low—which was simply to return home.

"You wouldn't want to be stuck back in time now, would you?" the man asked with a slight chuckle.

Erin shrugged. "I don't mind, as long as it's worth it."

"Besides," she added, "I could end up being the first woman to invent some kind of alternate power source for my belt."

Taking deep breaths, Erin tried to get rid of the fear creeping into her mind. She was heading off into uncertainty. It could be dangerous, but it also promised to be fun.

I've taken risks before, Erin thought to herself. This would just be one of them.

"No risk, no reward, as the old cliché goes," she muttered to herself.

It was soon time to go. The instructions echoed around her ears as she put on her goggles and strapped on her time belt. She also took with her a camera, to make memories of the wildest adventure she would ever have.

Once the time belt was activated, it opened up a portal of light through which Erin stepped. The period and era were carefully calibrated, and off she went.

CHAPTER 3

The light was blinding at first, and for a moment it felt like she couldn't breathe. Erin took a deep breath and exhaled once the light faded.

A rush of fresh air welcomed her to the new world. Her vision remained blurry for a few seconds, and her legs were wobbly. It felt as if she'd been spun around at light speed. At the same time, her body felt thin and weightless.

A minute later everything came into focus and Erin glanced up. She gasped when she saw the lush greenery surrounding her, and a majestic waterfall in the distance.

"Whoa, that's cool!" she said in awe. "I wonder where the dinosaurs are…" she was saying when the ground shook underneath her.

Letting out a sharp gasp, she ducked and rolled behind a rock, her shaky hands reaching for the forcefield device on her wrist. She activated it and shut her eyes, panting.

Almost immediately a roar echoed through the air with tremendous force.

"That's certainly a dino," she muttered with glee, took a deep breath and finally managed to get out of her hiding place.

She took out her camera, keeping her force field on, and began her exploration.

It took Erin a few minutes to realize that having her force field constantly on depleted her power reserves, and she knew she didn't want that.

Taking a deep breath, and reminding herself of the thrill of danger, she took off her force field and exposed herself to the dense Jurassic landscape.

"Time to find the locals," she quipped to herself.

She cut through huge bushes and soon found herself in the open. The sky was a flush of bright colours, and the air was crisp and cool. But the main attraction came up ahead. Majestic dinosaurs roamed around, some in herds while others slowly crept through the distant forest.

From where she squatted, binoculars in hand, she got a breathtaking view of a brachiosaurus. It seemed to have its head literally in the clouds as it drifted slowly through the terrain.

"No one's going to believe this!" Erin squealed in delight and took a few pictures. She also made a holographic recording for her book of memories. This would make a perfect addition.

She was still admiring the brachiosaurus, wondering what it would be like to climb on its back, when she heard the screech of a pterodactyl from up above.

"Holy shit!" she gasped and jumped back, cupping a hand above her forehead to shield her eyes from rays of sunlight. The pterodactyls seemed to fly in formation as they glided through the air.

"Okay, forget the brachiosaurus, I need to find out what riding one of those would feel like," she said. "I just hope I get the chance someday."

But until then, she thought; time for me to explore closer. She wanted to see the dinosaurs up close and get to understand their behaviours. She still had time—she checked to confirm—and adventure awaited her.

**

Erin spotted a herd of triceratops migrating across the plains. Fascinated by the creatures, she decided to follow them and observe their lives. They weren't aggressive—and she had her force field—so she felt safe enough to get close and take pictures.

"You guys look both majestic and cute," she complimented them. "And that's a hard look to pull off."

She sat on a rock and sketched one of the triceratopses. She'd narrow her eyes and take in its features, then smile as she put her stylus on her notepad and created the image. And in that entire time, she noticed how the triceratops stayed still, sometimes stealing glances at her.

It felt almost like it knew what she was doing and was trying not to ruin it.

"Wanna see what it looks like, big guy?" she asked with a smile, and it slowly moved closer to her.

She looked into its eyes as it got closer and felt oddly unafraid. Nothing in those shimmering orbs spelt danger. It was soon right next to her and she felt just how massive it was.

“Not sure I’d feel this relaxed around a Tyrannosaurus,” she joked and to her surprise, the triceratops shook its head and made a laugh-like whizzing sound.

“Wait a minute, you got my joke?” Erin asked, surprised. She’d read about dinosaurs in history books and humans had always believed they weren’t so smart. This triceratops laughed at her jokes and posed for her to sketch it.

And it was just so magical to look at. Erin sat with her knees together, placing the notepad on them. She wiggled her fingers and slowly reached out to the triceratops, careful not to scare it away.

“I came to experience your world,” she whispered.

Her hand was just an inch away from the triceratops’ face when the thundering roar of a T-rex shook the ground.

"Ah!" Erin screamed and fell off the rock when her new friend groaned and turned around, shoving her slightly.

The triceratops bellowed to the herd and hurried off to them. The roar continued, and soon the tyrannosaur showed up.

Of course she had seen that infamous saurian head, lined with teeth, in a thousand holos… but it looked so much bigger than any picture could have depicted. Erin stuffed her notepad back into her bag and got up, brushing the seat of her shorts.

She turned around and saw the herd of triceratops hurrying off. Swinging her gaze back to the T-rex, she gasped.

"It's going to kill them!"

She wasn't afraid for her safety but that of the peaceful triceratops. Tiny bits of rocks flew around her as the T-rex marched his heavy feet on the ground.

Thick clouds of dust formed around the herd now trying to escape.

Erin leaped over the rock and ran toward the herd. She was well aware of the T-rex behind her, now charging at the herd. Her heart raced at a mile a minute, and the voice of caution in her head warned her to stay out of this. It was nature, and some animals were made to get eaten.

She shook the thoughts away, running as fast as she could, her feet digging into the dirt and grass.

"Nothing's getting eaten on my watch."

A large shadow crossed over her, carrying with it a rush of wind. She slowed down a bit when the T-rex's large tail swept across her. She ducked and slid on the ground, splashing up water as she ran along the river bank.

The T-rex ignored her, easily outrunning her as it caught up with its prey.

Erin pressed a button on the device

strapped to her wrist, and then she zipped over to the front of the herd.

"Woah, can't believe that worked!" she panted, catching the herd storming toward her.

The T-rex snapped its large jaws at one of the triceratopses, narrowly missing it. While the herd ran toward her, Erin ran in the opposite direction, her eyes fixed on the T-rex while her fingers remained closed to her force field device.

The last triceratops ran past her—the one she'd been sketching—and suddenly stopped. It turned around and bellowed at Erin, calling on to her.

"I'll be fine!" she shouted. She turned around and saw that the herd were trapped by a mass of fallen rocks. They either had to turn back, toward the Tyrannosaurus, or wait for it to reach and devour them.

Erin held her breath, feeling the trembling beneath her feet. She was the only thing standing between the massive predator and the scampering herd. The T-rex was a few steps away now, roaring and showing off its menacing rows of knife-like teeth. She stood her ground, counting down in her head.

Just as it made to strike, she pushed down on the button.

“Don’t fail me now!” she screamed and shut her eyes, bracing for whatever was about to happen.

The forcefield shot out and spread over Erin and the herd. A massive force exploded from it, sending the T-rex stumbling back. It roared angrily and snapped its jaws on the force field, unable to break through.

It gave up after a few tries, let out a warning roar, and ran away.

Erin switched off the force field, noticing a drain of one bar from her time belt. She exhaled deeply, sweat trickling over her forehead, and fell to her knees.

“That was close,” she said to no one in particular.

But a familiar soft groan came up next to her. She turned and saw the triceratops. It rubbed its body on hers and offered her its snout as support.

“Thanks,” she said and put her arm around its face, her fingers grazing its front horn.

The triceratops moved up a bit, helping her to her feet. She giggled when it lifted her a little higher, getting her feet completely off the ground.

“You’re strong,” she laughed.

It made a soft sound and gently eased her back down. Erin looked around at the grateful herd. She waved at them.

“I hope everyone is cool?”

To her surprise, the herd responded with sounds of their own. She was certain now that they understood her, especially her friend.

"Where's my backpack?" Erin muttered to herself, looking around.

She retraced her steps, and the triceratops followed her.

"I hope the others won't be mad," she said softly, slowing down for the triceratops to catch up.

It groaned and she smiled. If only they could talk. It didn't matter though; somehow, she understood what it said, and it understood her.

She found her backpack partially soaked by the river. Everything was intact.

Bringing out her camera, she took a few pictures of the triceratops.

"Let's take one together," she said and put the camera on auto. It hovered in the air as if held by another human, and Erin skipped over to the side of the triceratops. She placed a hand on the side of its face and grinned.

The camera flashed a few times.

“You’re a natural,” she whispered to the creature.

She frowned when she noticed a fading pink scar on the side of the triceratops’ face. She gently moved her hand close to it, caressing the scar with the tip of her fingers.

“Got into a fight, huh?” she asked.

It cooed.

“A T-rex, I bet?”

It nodded and she stroked the spot around the scar, listening to the soft moan her triceratops made. She found it weird that she thought of this creature as hers, not like she owned it but as a close friend; something that was a part of her.

Like love at first sight, except with an ancient creature.

CHAPTER 4

It was a strangely satisfying feeling, bonding with the triceratops. Erin wouldn't let herself think of it as an 'it'.

"I'm going to give you a name," she said, sitting by the river, the triceratops nestling close to her. She enjoyed the feel of its body close to her, and the softness of its breathing.

"Let's call you…Cera," she giggled.

The triceratops did a playful shake of its head.

"Do you like it? I guess I'm not so great

at naming stuff, but I think Cera sounds beautiful."

She looked at Cera and touched his face, stroking it lovingly. "As beautiful as you are, and just as magical."

Cera's soft groans let her know he enjoyed her touch. She stood up and wrapped her arms around his head, embracing him tenderly.

"Beautiful horns," she whispered and traced each horn with her fingers. "Majestic."

A rumble of thunder drew their attention to the sky.

"Hmm, it wants to rain," Erin mumbled, watching thick rain clouds slowly roll out. "I better get going so I don't get caught in the downpour."

She embraced Cera again and then, after hesitating for a second, pressed her lips on the side of his face and kissed him.

Cera's eyes widened and he let out a deep rumble.

He likes that, Erin thought, closing her eyes as she tightened the embrace. She was certain Cera felt pleasure from her touches, but she wondered if it was right.

She peeled away from the embrace and started walking away. The winds picked up, cold and fast, and a few drops of rain touched her face and lips.

Cera's soft noise made her turn around.

"Still following me, huh?"

Cera grunted.

Erin smiled and urged him on. "Fine, come on then. I guess I could use the company."

They walked together, almost forgetting the rain increasing in intensity all around them. Then, a flash of lightning cut through the clouds, and the sky opened up. Erin squealed when the deluge of cold water hit her.

"Oh no, I'm going to be soaking wet!"

Cera communicated with Erin with soft groans and nudges from his head.

"You want me to get on?" she asked, and Cera groaned again, lowering himself.

Giggling, Erin got on Cera's back and rode the triceratops. She wasn't sure if it was the constant humping as it ran, but her body began to tremble in a pleasurable way as waves of tingles rushed through it, heating her up.

Cera took her to a large cave where they took shelter from the rain. She was drenched and her clothes stuck to her body, accentuating her curves, and giving a clear view of her perky nipples and pink areolas.

She let out a soft moan when Cera snuggled close to her, his body somehow warm. Were dinosaurs cold-blooded, or had that been proven a myth? In any case Cera felt warm as a stove.

"I'll better take off my clothes first," she said, her eyes moving to the entrance of the cave. Rain lashed down from all sides, the cold winds whistling. "We might be here a while, and I think that's perfect since I won't be alone."

She made a fire the old-fashioned way and stood next to the burning yellow and orange of its flames. Cera watched her take off her clothes, her body bent over and her hand slowly caressing down her sides. She wanted to put on a show for him—longed to keep him engaged and mesmerized, that majestic creature—so she did some kind of stripper routine.

Her cheeks turned pink when she took off her soaked top, freeing her breasts. Cera's attention remained unflinchingly on her. She saw the intrigue glowing in Cera's eyes, like he was gazing at a hypnotic item. That was compliment enough for her.

She took off all her clothes, her body heated by the fire and the rising desire rushing through her body. She did a seductive dance around the flames, drawing the triceratops' gaze.

Her breasts heaved and danced, her body moving to a slow, seductive rhythm. She skipped over to where the triceratops was and put her arms around him, letting her naked body rub against his.

The moment soon became intimate between them, heated by the strong need for each other's company. Erin closed her eyes and listened to his soft sounds as her hands moved over his body; and she shuddered to the rhythm, getting a rush of pleasure from the connection.

Their minds seemed to become connected when she held his face and looked into his eyes. At that moment, everything seemed to slow down. The howling winds became soft songs in the background, and the lashing rain a chorus weaving around them.

Erin kissed the triceratops again, slowly this time. The tip of her fingers brushed over the side of his face, teasing him, arousing an ancient need in him. The physical contact sent sparks flying between them; heating up the flames of desire eating up their bodies.

The more she held on to Cera, the more she felt the connection deepen. The triceratops lowered himself, eyes closed, and slid into a world of euphoric bliss. Moans and groans and soft gasps filled the air between them.

With each stroke from her fingers, and kiss from the dripping softness of her lips, the triceratops found itself nearing the explosive heights of ecstasy, unlike it had ever felt before.

He soon let out deep grunts of satisfaction, brushing his face against Erin's body. She straddled him, trembling from the tingles of pleasure, and held on tight. She let her body move to the rhythm of Cera's ecstasy, and soon became engulfed by it.

She bit her lips and shut her eyes, grinding faster, feeling her heated sex become sensitive with every motion. Her arms tightened around his body, her moans louder.

The fire burning cast a shadow of their bodies on the wall of the cave, intertwined like two mystical beings locked in a beautiful dance of love and pleasure and deep primeval lust.

CHAPTER 5

Erin opened her eyes when she felt something warm brushing over her skin. It aroused her, the way it caressed her body. At first, she thought she was having an erotic dream, then her vision became focused on Cera and she smiled. Her eyes lit up, and then they crinkled at the corners.

"What are you doing to me," she giggled when he breathed on her skin and moved his face low between her legs. She moaned and parted them, caressing his face and guiding his tongue down to the aching spot between her legs.

She loved how the triceratops sparked

this desire in her, the way he made her body tremble. She surrendered herself to him, complete naked. Cera moved his face slowly along her body, brushing over her chest, tickling her erect nipples. He was careful because he knew how fragile Erin was; she saw that in his eyes.

Spreading her legs wider, she let him lick her.

"Oh, yes!" She moaned and felt a rush. It was like having a psychedelic trip, the way the sweet tingles exploded through her body.

Cera groaned and only pushed his tongue deeper, fiercely swiping at her wetness. Erin held on to his face with one hand, squeezing her right tit with the other. Her body arched forward, her legs still parted, and soon she began to tremble harder.

Erin couldn't get enough of Cera and the immense sexual pleasure she enjoyed with him. She knew she'd have to leave someday, so she wanted to enjoy it as much as possible.

They stayed together in the cave, enjoying their intimacy away from the world outside.

While Cera slept, Erin crept up to him.

She grinned and placed her hand on his body, feeling the slow rhythm of his breaths, and the soft groans he made.

It was her turn to wake him up with wild sexual feelings. She moved her hand along his massive body as if making a painting, tapping slowly with the tip of her fingers.

She'd spent enough time with Cera to know where he liked to be touched and kissed; the places that made him stiffen from pleasure.

She let her hand continue trailing over the side of his body, moving down to his rear. He stirred slightly and groaned when she moved lower. His breathing became faster, and his eyes opened slowly.

Erin glanced at him, sliding her hand under his tummy.

"Did I wake you?" She asked in a teasing, sexy voice. Cera groaned and breathed deeply.

She moved her fingers under him and rubbed him slowly.

Her eyes widened when she felt the hard shaft underneath his body. Before now, she'd been curious but hesitant about it. Now, listening to his soft groans and feeling the heat intensify in her body, she knew she had to explore.

She grazed his shaft with her fingers, moaning softly. Cera jerked a bit from the touch and she quickly placed a hand on his body, cooing softly.

He relaxed and let out a peaceful groan. She knelt next to him, the air in the cave brushing between her already wet pussy--her juices trickled down, and she ached to be touched and tasted again.

But first, she thought with a sly grin and clasped her hand around the growing shaft. The hardness throbbed in her grasp, and sticky fluids trickled out when she stroked him a little. Cera's groans increased as she continued stroking his shaft, her hand underneath his body.

The more she made that jacking motion with her hand, the hotter she felt. Cera's shaft soon grew long and hard, twitching as she tightened her grip around it.

A prehistoric cock, she couldn't stop herself from thinking. *What would this feel like inside me?* she wondered.

Cera's groans increased and he stirred a few times, his body shaking and his eyes wide open. The sounds of pleasure echoed around the cave walls and it only encouraged Erin to keep going.

Still on her knees, Erin slid her free hand between her legs.

"Oh, that feels so good, Cera!" she

moaned when she slipped two fingers between her wet folds, her other hand still frantically stroking Cera.

Her hand was soon smeared with Cera's sticky fluids. He let out a long groan and his shaft throbbed, and he spurted his fluids all over her hand.

Erin shifted closer to Cera and kissed his face, panting.

"That's the biggest load I've ever seen," she giggled and held up her hand, showing the sticky fluids dripping down her fingers.

Feeling naughty, she slapped the hand between her legs and rubbed the sticky fluids between her legs, moaning and shivering.

She laid on her back, inviting Cera over. His breathing was still deep and he was a bit slow—still recovering from the pleasures she'd given him.

He nudged his nose between her legs while her fingers dipped in and out of her hole. She raised her legs and Cera stretched out his tongue, running the tip along her anal hole and up to her wet pussy.

“Ooh, that’s…good,” she gasped.

Cera grunted and carefully got her to roll to her side until she laid face down.

Giggling, her legs spread wide, she asked him what he was doing. She wasn’t afraid of getting crushed by his weight—and he was careful not to step on her, so that made her feel safe.

Cera grunted and pressed his hard shaft down on her.

“Ooh!” Erin moaned when she felt the hard end of his shaft poking between her cheeks. She pushed her hips up, clenching her fists, and let out soft moans as Cera humped her.

He was huge, so he just brushed his shaft over her ass and pussy, increasing his pace as she moaned and grinded into his thrusts. The contact was electric. She bit her lip and gasped, feeling herself getting closer. Her orgasm was more intense than any she'd ever had. She stretched her legs and her body stiffened as the hard shaft continued brushing up and down her slit. It soon throbbed and Cera groan, spurting his fluids all over her ass and pussy.

She turned around, body drenched in sweat, panting and catching her breath. Keeping her legs open, she managed to grab hold of his shaft and milked it with a few strokes, letting the last few drops coat her swollen lips. Cera let out a contented moan, communicating his satisfaction to Erin. "There's going to be more where that came from," she promised with a soft giggle.

She rested her body on Cera, eyes closed, enjoying the moment and wishing she could have more of it. They stayed that way for a long time, bodies touching, breathing almost rhythmically, the passion and electricity surging between them.

**

Erin loved the way Cera looked at her when she didn't have any clothes on. The way his eyes sparkled let her know he appreciated the beauty of her body. She laughed when she realized just how silly people would think it was when she told them about this empathic connection one could have with dinosaurs, and how they felt pleasure and dished it out just as well.

They went over to the beach side, under the glow of a perfect full moon. Their bodies glimmered from the light, and the waters sparkled and glowed. It was the perfect atmosphere for a sexually-charged encounter with her favorite triceratops.

She walked along the beachside, letting the foamy water wash over her feet. At a certain point, she took a couple of steps into the water and let the waves wash over her body. Cera's arched his head and rushed in, perhaps think something bad had happened to her.

She popped her head out, gasping for air and grinning at Cera.

"I'm fine," Erin laughed, kneeling on the water. She let the waves bathe her, making her body glisten, and grabbed her breasts with both hands. She pursed her lips and swayed her hips slowly, doing a sensual dance.

"Come on then," she beckoned on Cera and he stepped into water, bringing his face closer to Erin. She reached out slowly and touched him. Then, without warning, she splashed water on the triceratops.

He let out a playful sound and took a few steps. Erin got out of the water, her body dripping wet, and put her arms around the triceratops. She pulled him into a tight embrace, closing her eyes and moaning softly at the body contact. It amazed her how turned on she could get just from touching the dinosaur.

Cera grunted a few times and shook its body, urging her to do what she did best: caress his body, and touch him in that slow, sensual, teasing way.

She whispered soft words to him and moved her hand under his face, stroking gently. As usual, Cera's body reacted to the fingers tracing over his skin. He shuddered and groaned; his mouth slightly open—even drooling.

Cera remained still while Erin moved slowly along the side, the tip of her fingers moving up and down. She finally moved her hands under his belly, grazing her fingers over his crotch. She felt that throb once she touched him; an awakening of desire.

She slipped her hand between her legs while stroking Cera, letting her fingers slide between the wet folds of her heated sex. She squeezed her hand around Cera's crotch and began to slowly jerk him off, while dipping her fingers in and out of her dripping pussy.

Their collective sounds of pleasure filled the air—the moans and grunts mixing into a tense echo shaking through the atmosphere. Erin got on her knees again,

She got on all fours and shook her hips, teasing Cera with her pink, wet pussy, the juices trickling down her legs. He moved closer to her, brushing his tongue over her lips. Erin trembled as waves of tingles rushed over her body. She steeled herself as Cera got in position, the tip of his hard member poking at her hole.

Erin took in a deep breath and bit her lips, moaning aloud as she felt him stretch her and slide deeper. The squishy sound of his cock rubbing her wetness was arousing. He pushed in slowly, making sure she was alright.

Gasping, Erin dug hand fingers into the sand in and her body pushed forward as he went in deep. The hotness of his breath filled her body, and his deep groans as he began to move frantically in and out of her.

Each thrust from that triceratops cock sent shivers through her body, pushing her fast toward a fiery orgasm. She backed into Cera's deep strokes, arching her back and grinding into him. She felt herself getting stretched and filled up, her pelvis taking a hit.

How long did it take? She wasn't certain, but her moans only became sharper until she felt that ecstatic shudder. Her pussy gripped him tighter and she shut her eyes, flattening her face on the sand, shaking from her orgasm.

The triceratops continued humping until he filled her up with his fluids. He pulled out slowly and globs of cum trickled out from between her legs, her body flushed and writhing.

Erin laid on the sand and Cera moved close to her, letting his body rest protectively close to hers. She shifted closer and rested her head on him, her body still hot despite the cool night air. She felt the tingles between her legs, a sweet reminder of her evening. She closed her eyes and sighed softly. It sure had been a sizzling adventure, and the best part of it was the fact that there would always be more.

For now, though, she was spent and just needed a good rest with Cera next to her.

CHAPTER 6

Erin stayed with Cera for a week. It felt like an eternity, those seven days; and somehow, it also felt like seven hours. Not long enough. Cera felt her need to explore, so he took her everywhere.

They had a few close calls, like the time she'd almost fallen off a cliff, but Cera was always close by to save her. They created a lot of memories, all of which she saved.

"I'm going to be looking at these pictures for a long, long time," she whispered to Cera. They always stayed together at night. She'd be completely nude, her body resting on his.

The feeling was addictive, she quickly realized—having that connection with such a timelost creature.

The charge on her belt ran low on the seventh day. She knew that time was running out, but she tried to ignore it and not think about leaving Cera alone in this harsh world.

They spent their final hours together walking along the beach, taking in the beautiful sunset, and catching the echoes of various predators in the distance.

It was time to go.

"This has been the best week of my life," she said, embracing the triceratops. Who would have thought she'd bond with a prehistoric creature; and not just bond, but have a real connection.

She felt his sadness when she moved back, making her preparations for departure. It made her realize one thing: she definitely had to come back again. She wasn't sure what it would cost, and if they'd let her use the time machine again, but she had so much to discover about this world. And she was ready to let people know how deeply developed these creatures were; how much more intelligent than previously thought.

Erin gave the triceratops one last embrace, and a deep kiss, and opened up her time portal. She stepped through it, eyes still on her strange lover, and bade one final farewell.

My Boyfriend is a Plesiosaur

Erin was set for another adventure. There was something exciting about the Jurassic era. Perhaps it had to do with the perceived danger, but she was certain she wanted another mind-blowing sensual adventure in that time period. Her heart fluttered as many exciting thoughts popped up in her head. She had a feeling that this adventure would be even more exciting than the first.

It was almost impossible to settle on which majestic dinosaur to have her adventure with, but her mind was soon made up after spotting the graceful plesiosaur gliding in the depths of the ocean.

I have to be down there, she told herself. She wanted to soothe the lonely creature and share a wonderful experience with it.

A mad idea, people thought, but she was soon ready to delve deep into the ocean. She had her force fields and rebreathers, and a tight-fitting sexy underwater suit. The plesiosaur was intelligent enough to get aroused by her beautiful, sexy body—and she knew that.

Erin made sure her gears were set, then she jumped into the ocean. Bubbles rose around her as she swam deeper, and the sparkling rays of light reflecting against the blue ocean soon became dim trickles.

Minutes passed and it got darker around her. She checked her locator and saw that she was getting closer. Her anticipation rose, and she couldn't hold back from smiling as she got even nearer to the plesiosaur.

I can almost feel the tremors, she thought. And she was right.

A moment later, the bright beam of

her flashlight exposed the long neck of the plesiosaur. It swam around her, humming deeply, and slowly rose in front of her.

Erin felt overwhelmed by the sight of the creature. She reached out her arm slowly and it hesitated and backed off, sweeping bubbles over her. Using a special device, she boomed out sound waves through the ocean. The plesiosaur turned around and swam to her. Its long neck curved around her slowly and she reached out and grazed its body with her hand.

She moved her hand slowly, making light strokes over its neck, then she swam closer and wrapped her arms around it. The creature closed its eyes and let out soft hums, enjoying her embrace. Erin moved up a bit and brought her face close to its face, their eyes locked. She felt an instant connection at that moment, the creature's soft sounds floating around her.

Erin held it close and tenderly, moving her hand all over the length of its neck—as far as her hand could reach—and then it kicked a little and got her on its back.

They swam around the ocean, taking in the beauty of the ocean—the colorful coral, and the mass of seaweed dancing to the rhythm of the ocean waves. The creature swam up to the surface and took Erin over to the side of the beach. She took off her rebreather and let loose her hair.

Taking off her swim suit, she bared her naked body before the creature. She could feel it calling her over, craving her touch and the feel of her body. She smiled and obliged, letting its face cradle her bosom.

She moaned softly and felt the coolness of its body on hers. She warmed it up with her embrace, sliding her body up and down, and then straddled it again.

A slight chill rushed up her spine when her body made contact with the plesiosaur. She moved faster, grinding herself on it, clinging tight and caressing slowly with her finger. She bucked to the side and fell off its body. She giggled when she hit the ground, and the plesiosaur groaned and stretched its head close to her.

She was soaking wet at this point... and no, it wasn't just the water.

She pursed her lips and moaned when the plesiosaur rested its head between her legs, breathing down on her. The heat against her wetness made her tremble and squeal out in delight. She arched her hips and slid her hand over the back of its head, humping it.

Her moans grew louder and faster, her grip on it tighter. Her body soon trembled as waves of pleasure hit her, and she pressed her back on the sand and closed her eyes. After a moment, she managed to get up and climbed onto the plesiosaur's back, resting her weight on it.

She felt its contentment at having her around, and smiled when it moaned at her hands stroking its body. She used both hands and massaged its body, stroking sensually. The soft groans became louder and the plesiosaur moved its body in response to her touch.

"You're enjoying this, aren't you?" she whispered, and it moaned. She continued massaging and touching intimately until its body stiffened and shivered, and she knew she'd hit the right spot.

Its moans softened again and it closed its eyes, thankful for the experience.

They stayed together for a while, dipping in and out of the water, enjoying the warm breezes and the until the sun went down. She stood right in front of it and pressed her hands gently on its face, gazes locked. Moving closer, she touched her lips on it and kissed it gently.

"Time to go," she whispered and it let out a soft whine.

Putting on her rebreather again, Erin slid back into the water with the plesiosaur. She held on tight as they settled in the depths of the ocean, enjoying each other's company, connecting beyond words. She felt its loneliness drift away while holding on.

She couldn't stay underwater forever, so she kissed the plesiosaur and whispered sweet words to it. It looked somber when she tried to leave, but another kiss to its face—and a tight embrace—brightened everything.

Once back in the surface, wrapped in the afterglow of her sensual experience, Erin activated the time belt. Off to her next adventure.

Mile High Pterodactyl Club

The heavy screeches overhead sent a pulse of excitement through Erin's body. She pushed back a heavy branch and pulled out a binocular, aiming the lens at the sky.

Her heart raced wildly when she caught a glimpse of one of them. The more she stared at it gliding through the clouds, the hotter she became. She was already so taken by the sight that she had no idea when she moved her hand over her chest, brushing her fingers over her hardened nipples.

Grinning, she put down the binoculars and squinted. There it was, its heavy wings beating majestically.

"So close," she muttered to herself and

trudged forward, slicing through blades of grass, each minute taking her closer to her target. This was going to be one of the best experiences ever, better than all her other sexy time-travel adventures.

If only she could get close enough.

Erin followed the screeching sounds and went deeper into the jungle. The earth trembled around her as a loud roar echoed in the distance.

"A giganotosaurus," she muttered to herself, a soft chuckle escaping her lips. She tapped a watch-like device on her wrist, securing herself in a force field. Nothing could harm her now.

She hastened her steps, running through the thick brush. Her eyes went up to the sky and she saw it again—the reason she'd traveled back in time to this prehistoric era. The ground elevated as she ran, and she soon found herself ascending up a mountain.

"Okay, this is crazy," she panted.

"You're going to lose them!"

The screeches grew quieter as the creatures flew farther away.

With a frantic push of a button on the device on her wrist, the space before her ripped apart and she stepped through, teleporting herself straight to the peak of the mountain.

She felt her body stretching and thinning as she warped through space, and then a splash of light hit her face when she burst out above the mountain. Perfect, she thought for a second. Except she'd somehow overshot it and found herself free falling through the sky.

Sharp winds slapped against her face as she tried to reach for her teleportation device.

Suddenly, a heavy screech echoed around her and a pterodactyl swooped in from underneath her. She clung to it, her heart beating fast, and slowly opened her eyes.

This is happening, she thought, embracing the creature tightly. The warmth of its body spread through to hers as she clung to it, and it let out a deep groan.

"Thank you," Erin whispered to it, stroking the back of its neck with the tip of her fingers. It let out soft sounds and she smiled. "You're enjoying this, aren't you?" she asked in a soft, sensual tone.

The pterodactyl responded with a slight shake, and more groans. Erin bit her lips and carefully straddled the creature while in mid-flight. This was an experience she'd always wanted to try and somehow, she'd fallen straight into it.

The humans from the future had discovered that dinosaurs were more intelligent and sensual than previously thought. Now, it was a wild experience daredevils like her sought out: deep sexual encounters with dinosaurs.

Erin was certain no one had experienced such with a pterodactyl before.

The pterodactyl couldn't speak, but she knew it could understand her, feel her touches and respond to them.

It flew higher into the clouds, giving Erin a view of the splash of colors below.

"It feels like it's just us up here," she whispered. She felt her shorts riding up her crotch as she clasped her thighs together, adjusting herself on top of its back.

It let out a soft moan and glided steadily.

"Don't worry, I'm not afraid of falling," she said and moved upward, putting her arms around its long neck. The thrill only increases with more danger, she always told herself.

Erin placed her hand flat on its neck, feeling the subtle pulse rushing through its body. She caressed gently, moaning softly, and smiled when it responded with a shiver and a slight moan.

The low sounds of pleasure increased as she caressed its neck, letting her know it was enjoying it. She kept going, unbothered by the wind against her face. She stretched her legs and flattened her body and pressed her huge breasts on its back, slowly writhing on top of the creature.

Her hands continued stroking and caressing, and her moans drifted around the creature's face. She shut her eyes and held tight to the pterodactyl, her body moving to its rhythm as it flew lower. She could feel the vibrations rushing through its body as they were locked in a sensual embrace; feel its pleasure mount and near eruption.

And at the same time, it sent waves of tingles through her body. They were wrapped as one in the moment, gliding the clouds, experiencing the height of pleasure.

An idea popped up in her head. She sat up and took off her top, letting her boobs bounce freely. Then, she carefully slid off her shorts.

Her nipples were harder than ever, and she was soaking wet between her legs. She stuffed her clothes in her backpack and embraced the pterodactyl, rubbing her bare body against its. It must have felt the difference because it moaned and shook its head, weaving through the sky.

Erin could barely stand when her feet finally touched the ground. She giggled and wrapped her arms around the pterodactyl again, once again teasing it by sliding her hand down its belly and stroking it. She loved the way it moaned and shivered when she touched it, and the way her body also heated up in response.

“We’re going to have to do this again someday,” she whispered and opened up a portal, ready to get off to her next sexy adventure.

I wonder who’ll be the first to spot the naked time traveler with a backpack, she thought slyly.

A Carnotaurus for Christmas

Erin sighed and stared out the window. It was Christmas eve and everything felt… normal.

Ordinary's more the word I'm looking for, she thought. She longed for her time travelling adventures; to be able to travel back in time and see the world before all this. To experience again the marvels of prehistory.

She sighed again and moved away from the window.

"Who cares if I breached a few regulations?" she muttered to herself. "No one else wanted to test out the time traveling device but me. They should be happy I spent all those time charges leaping through various prehistoric periods."

She fell on a couch, sulking. *Why'd they have to ban me, anyway? I mean, a slap on the wrist would have been okay.*

But then she knew that this wasn't her first warning. Maybe she deserved it.

She was still sulking when a package arrived for her. It was unmarked, but had a small note attached to it.

"What's this?" she said under her breath, reading the inscription on the note.

'Have fun and a Merry Christmas.'

"A secret admirer, hmm?"

Shrugging, she opened the package and her eyes widened. At first, she thought it was a gimmick. On close inspection she became sure of what it was: a charged-up time belt.

She took a cautious look around her apartment, hoping no one was spying on her—and that this was some cruel prank—and then locked her door.

Without wasting a moment, she activated the time belt and found herself drifting through the fabric of infinity once more.

**

Erin found herself dumped right inside the den of an adult Carnotaurus. It took her a few seconds to get used to her surrounding—the blinding lights faded and a rush of air blew against her face—and she found herself staring straight at the creature.

Having a couple of time-travelling encounters with prehistoric creatures had sparked enough interest in her to know a lot about the various species...

The carnotaurus growled when it saw her. It tilted its large head to the side, focusing its eyes on her.

Erin knew what to do. She held out her hands, taking two steps forward.

“Hey big guy,” she whispered, a charming smile on her face. “I’m not going to hurt you; just a friend who’s a little lost.”

The ground shook when it also moved forward, sweeping its massive body from side to side.

Erin moved to the side, pressing her body against the wall of its lair. She steadied herself when the carnotaurus moved closer, its face an inch away from hers.

“See, just a friend,” she whispered, slowly moving one hand close to its face.

It snorted its hot breath at her face, inching back nervously.

“Shhh, shhh,” she hushed it, bravely placing her hand on its face. She felt its breathing become soft, even gasping. And soon it relaxed.

Erin held its gaze while moving her hand along the side of its face, stroking tenderly.

"And you're lonely, aren't you?" She whispered, glancing at the lair. "All alone."

It groaned and closed its eyes, and she knew it felt emotions.

Looking into those eyes formed a connection between them. She felt that familiar spark; a longing for this creature.

Realizing she wasn't a threat, the carnotaurus moved back slowly and made a pleasant sound.

"You're welcoming me? Why, thank you," she said gleefully.

It was hot inside the lair so she took off her shirt. It was becoming a habit, showing off her body whenever she time traveled, but she loved the charmed look they gave her.

The creature was soon all over her, moaning sensually and caressing her body with its head. She caressed it back, using her fingers expertly.

The creature responded intelligently to her words. Sure, it couldn't speak, but she hardly felt that gap. She touched every part of its body, exploring with the tip of her fingers, and the softness of her lips.

She soon realized how incredibly dexterous its relatively small vestigial claws were.

It would moan each time she whispered something sweet to it.

"You're a special one, aren't you?" She'd coo and kiss it, and it'd vibrate and moan. Her body was soon slippery with sweat as her body heated up--both from the temperature, and her arousal.

It lowered itself when she asked it to, and Erin straddled the creature. It was a bit awkward, but that didn't matter when she rode it--grinding herself into its body, grasping tight and letting her moans rip through the air.

She knew the creature reached its sexual climax when it let out a deep groan and shuddered.

They spent many hours together in its lair. Erin talked to it about her world, getting responsive sounds. She'd pause occasionally and embrace and kiss it, stroking the side of its face.

The carnotaurus must have been an outsider among the other predators, but it had her now and she made it happy.

It was time to go once again. Erin knew she shouldn't let the time belt die on her; that'd mean staying trapped back in time. She was still banned from time travelling, so this was technically illegal.

She embraced her new friend, getting that electric jolt she so enjoyed each time she bonded with these creatures.

"I hope you won't be so lonely anymore," she said and it let out a soft moan.

She smiled and kissed it. "Of course, you won't. You're a big boy."

She said goodbye and travelled back to her time, beaming and feeling fulfilled.

Am I addicted to this now? She wondered, when she saw just how much she glowed.

Back in her apartment, she went back to the opened box she'd tossed to the side. Taking the note, she flipped it over and read it again.

A phone number glowed on the corner, imprinted in gold.

She took her terminal and sent a message to her mystery admirer, smiling slyly. Whomever they were, they'd made her happy.

'A VERY Merry Christmas indeed!' she sent back.

My Sexy Supersaurus

Erin got another package from her secret admirer. It had been a couple of weeks since the last package—and the beautiful Christmas present that came with it—so she was excited about this one.

The first thing she reached for was the note attached to the package. She wanted to surprise herself later, but for now she wanted to see if her secret admirer had revealed who they were.

The note was made in the same handwriting as the last one—she'd pored over it for days—and the words written were brief.

Look inside the box.

"Hmm, okay," she giggled and knelt by

the package. She tore open the wrapping, her heart beating fast, and, after taking a deep breath, opened it.

Her smile faded into a deep frown when she saw nothing but a card at the bottom of the box. No time belt—she'd been shying away from the thought, but she really hoped it would be another time belt... Erin was still technically on the naughty list for chronosphere use, due to some over-exuberant misadventures in the Cretaceous era.

"It's just a heavy box," she sighed and took out the glossy black card. She narrowed her eyes and read out the inscriptions. It was a VIP pass to Offworld, a super exclusive club. Her secret admirer had to be rich…super rich. That explained how he was able to obtain the time belt, she concluded.

This would be her chance to meet this person, and perhaps thank them for the gift. And maybe, just maybe, she could find out more about where the time belt had come from.

Erin arrived at the club and was let in immediately. She felt like she was part of this elite class, and that was all thanks to her secret admirer. The pulsing neon setting only made her curious. A man in a crisp dark suit walked up to her. He looked like one of those security type dudes.

"This way, please," he said and led her upstairs to a room.

The man stopped by the door and turned to Erin.

"She's waiting," he said and the door slid open.

"Wait, she?" Erin asked before stepping inside.

The room was a bit dark at first, then the lights flickered to life.

"Just being a little dramatic," a female voice came up. A busty woman stepped out and smiled beautifully at Erin.

"I've been waiting for you," she said, opening her arms wide as she pulled Erin into an embrace.

"You're my secret admirer?" Erin asked in surprise, feeling the woman's breasts against her body.

"And a huge fan," the woman added. "I'm Kim."

Kim was attractive—nice curves, a beautiful round face with glossy lips and deep blue eyes; and those tits!

Erin was about to introduce herself when Kim smiled and pressed a finger on her lips.

"I already know you."

She snapped her fingers and holographic screens appeared around them. It was all the images and videos of Erin on her adventures with the pterodactyl, triceratops and more. Erin's eyes widened when she saw it all, while Kim stared in awe. She's seen this so many times, Erin noted.

"All your sexy adventures with those dinosaurs," Kim's voice bubbled. "I never knew such creatures could be so…intimate."

She turned to Erin and whispered. "I have to admit, I've touched myself a couple of times just picturing myself out there with you."

Erin blushed, unable to take her eyes off the screens.

"I didn't know they recorded my adventures," she muttered. "That explains the ban."

"They suck, but they aren't going to stop us now."

Erin looked away from the screen. "Us?"

Kim's eyes lit up. "Oh, yes! I've always wondered what a sexy time-travelling adventure would be like, and I dream about going on one with you. Now's our chance."

The excitement caught on. “Really?”

Kim winked at her. “You and I, and whatever marvelous creature we come across.”

She moved close to Erin, their lips almost touching. Her voice was low and soft…lustful. “A steamy encounter with you is just what I need right now.”

Then her eyes sparkled again and she pulled Erin into a special room. “We don’t have to waste any time! Let’s do it now.”

“Like, right now?”

Kim bit her lips and giggled. “I’ve got time belts for the both of us.”

Unable to contain herself, Erin squeezed Kim in her arms. “We’re going to have the sexiest adventure yet, and you’re gonna love it!”

Kim gazed into her eyes, keeping her hands on Erin’s ass. “I love it already.”

They put on their time belts and Erin felt a new thrill at the idea of bringing someone along. She was like the master, and her secret admirer Kim would be the eager student. She couldn't wait.

"You don't have anything to worry about this time," Kim said. "Our time travelling is not sanctioned by any official bodies. We can do whatever the hell we want. I've got the money."

"Sounds like a dream," Erin giggled.

"Oh, it isn't a dream, baby girl. It's very much real."

They packed up their supplies in a backpack and activated their time belts. Holding hands, they stepped into the portal and let the light spread around their bodies.

**

Erin watched amusedly as Kim tried to get herself oriented. She blinked rapidly and wobbled on her feet, so Erin had to hold her steady.

"You'll get used to it eventually," Erin assured her, definitely feeling like a master now.

They took in the lush environment, and Erin's excitement exploded through her body. She was back again, ready for some sexy adventures.

She took Kim's hand, now in a place of her own, and they trudged down a path. Using a map, Kim was able to locate a dinosaur.

"I don't usually use a map," Erin pointed out. "I just like to surprise myself."

"Okay, let's do your thing," Kim said and switched off the map.

**

Erin's eyes widened and she grinned when she spotted it.

"That's a big guy," she said, pointing straight at the huge supersaurus. It towered over the foliage, gently grazing on the treetops.

"Hard to miss," Kim said, her voice shaky with excitement and nervousness.

Erin took her hand.

"Let's go have fun," she said.

Kim hesitated for a moment, looking nervous.

"Uhm, is that a good idea? He looks pretty big," she said.

Erin turned to her, smiling.

"We're cool, alright," she assured her. "We've got a force field in case things get out of control, and we can always travel back home."

"No!" Kim cut in. "I don't want to travel back home so soon. I came here to have a steamy encounter, and I'm not leaving without it."

"That's the spirit," Erin said gleefully.

The supersaurus growled and they glanced up. Its long neck was stretched in their direction, its eyes fixed on them.

"He's got eyes on us now," Erin said, looking at Kim. "How are your seduction skills?"

Kim's eyes sparkled. "Top notch!"

"Remember, these creatures are very empathic," Erin explained, already drawing the dinosaur's attention by taking slow steps to the side. "And sensual," she added with a wink.

They came out in the wide-open grassland and the supersaurus lowered its long neck. Kim was right behind Erin, watching in awe as she moved closer and touched the dinosaur's face.

"You're so beautiful!" she gasped.

It groaned and tilted its head to the side, leaning into Erin's soft hand. She moved her face closer while caressing it, and kissed it softly.

"I'm Erin," she said, still speaking sensually and stroking its face with her fingers. It groaned as if trying to say what its name was. Erin smiled and held it close, feeling the warmth on her skin, and the occasional shiver along its neck.

"I've got a friend," she said, turning around. They supersaurus looked up and stared at Kim. It looked hesitant at first, turning to Erin and groaning softly.

Erin laughed and gestured for Kim to get closer.

"She's just as lovely as I am," she said. Kim stood next to Erin, eyes wide at the sight of the magnificent supersaurus up close.

Erin took Kim's hand and gently raised it.

"Relax," she whispered, holding Kim's gaze. She guided her hand onto the dinosaur's face and slowly helped her make smooth motions from side to side.

The dinosaur moaned and closed its eyes, enjoying the touch from both hands.

"Just relax and feel the magic," Erin moaned into Kim's ear, letting go of her hand.

Kim smiled and exhaled deeply, letting go of her nervousness. She'd never been so close to such a creature before, let alone touched one.

She soon got into it and moved her hands faster. The dinosaur brought its face closer and she wrapped her arms around its neck, placing her lips close to its face. She kissed gently, sliding her tongue over its skin, tasting it.

The moans and soft groans became louder, and Kim's body shivered. Erin wasn't going to be left out. This truly was a chance of a lifetime: sharing that special sensual connection with another human who felt the same way.

Erin giggled when the dinosaur licked

her face, grunting a little.

"He's communicating with us," Kim gushed. "It's almost as if I know just what he wants, and what he's trying to say."

"You're getting into it now," Erin said.

"Let's ride him," she said excitedly.

She stood then in front of the supersaurus, while its head lowered just enough to get more caressing. "We want to get on you, big guy," Kim said.

It slowly moved its tail to the side and Kim's lips widened. She turned to Erin and took her hand, pulling her to the side of the supersaurus. They climbed up its tail and careful got on its back.

The supersaurus grunted after they'd gotten on, probably asking if they were alright.

"We're good," Erin said.

Kim had her hand around Erin's back while Erin held on to the supersaurus. The dinosaur took slow steps around the lush grassland, past a large body of water.

They got to a secluded spot where the ladies decided to get down and have some real fun.

“I’ve never had a threesome like this before,” Kim said, laughing. She was already taking off her clothes, making eye contact with the supersaurus. “I think he’s checking me out.”

Erin giggled. “They’re very sensual,” she reminded Kim. “More than you’d ever think.”

Kim tossed all her clothes aside and ran over to the dinosaur, rubbing her nude body on it. She moaned softly and caressed it. Erin joined in also, loving how Kim was getting into the entire idea. She placed one hand on Kim, touching her body intimately and letting her hand stray lower and lower.

The ladies lay on the grass, and the supersaurus moved closer to them, keeping its head close to the action.

"Let's put on a little show," Erin whispered into Kim's ear.

Kim moaned and laid on her back, spreading her legs invitingly wide. She watched as the supersaurus inched his head close in between her legs, thrusting its nozzle up her wet folds.

Shivering, she shut her eyes and parted her lips. The hot sensation in between her legs sent a new kind of thrill rushing through her body; an addictive kind. The wild thumping in her chest increased when the dinosaur's shadow fell over her—a mix of fear and pleasure.

"You're safe, don't worry," Erin whispered and kissed her. She crawled over to the side of the supersaurus' neck and also kissed its face, whispering something to it. The dinosaur groaned softly and gently teased Kim with hot blasts of air from its snout.

Erin slid her hand between Kim's legs, moving her fingers over her swollen lips. "You're wet," she said, feeling the juices trickling over her fingers.

"I know," Kim giggled. She thrust her hips forward, grinding her wetness into the face of the supersaurus, while pressing her lips on Kim's boobs. She flicked Kim's erect nipples with her tongue and gently sucked on them, keeping her hand between her legs.

"I'm not sure I can handle more of this," Kim squealed, shaking from the intense combination of having the dinosaur teasing her with its face—rubbing its hard skin over her body—and Erin's lips working on her nipples.

She locked her legs around the dinosaur's head, panting, and continued grinding into it until she felt that familiar explosion of pleasure. Erin's lips smacked when she let go of Kim's glistening nipples. She ran her tongue over her body, moving down to her thighs. She stroked the side of the dinosaur's face while it increased the back-and-forth motion of its head. Kim moaned and screamed, her body shaking. She dug her fingers into the ground, pulling out strands of grass as her body vibrated from the waves of pleasure hitting her. She tried to hold on to Erin, squeezing one arm around her neck, riding the wave of her intense orgasm.

She finally exhaled deeply and closed her eyes, her body relaxing a little.

The supersaurus groaned softly and lifted its head, drawing closer to Erin who swept her tongue over the wetness on its face. She smiled and kissed it again, tasting Kim's juices. She wrapped her arms around its neck and straddled it.

With a simple tug the dinosaur had her high up in the air. Erin squealed excitedly, hanging on—locking her thighs and moaning as her pussy made contact with the dinosaur's skin. She rested her face on its body, planting soft kisses on it while she moved her hip back and forth, rubbing her aching wet sex on the dinosaur.

She rode faster, her moans getting louder, until her pussy clenched and she creamed all over the dinosaur's body. It lowered its head and she slid until the ground, panting, leaving her legs wide open.

Kim remained on the ground trying to catch her breath, and Erin soon joined her.

The massive dinosaur grunted impatiently and nudged them with its snout, as if to tell them it wasn't done yet.

"Let's give him a sexy double treatment," Kim suggested, getting on her knees. She still felt the hard contact between her legs, and the aftershock of her orgasm.

They gestured for the dinosaur to come closer. He obliged and stretched his long neck over to them. His body was so massive they were certain it would take more than two of them to successfully pleasure him, but they were willing to try.

Erin knelt on one side, her body smooth

and sweaty; and Kim stayed on the other side. They both held on to the dinosaur's face, working with their hands and fingers. They used the tip of their fingers to tickle and caress, arousing the creature.

Still with their hands on its body, they moved their faces close together and kissed deeply. And then, turned to face the dinosaur and kissed him at the same time. The dinosaur reacted with a pleasant groan, pushing his head forward, asking for more.

Hands trailed under his neck, stroking his sensitive body until his groans grew louder and he swayed his long neck from side to side.

"You think he has a cock?" Kim wondered aloud and Erin shrugged, pursing her lips. They went under the dinosaur. He knew they were there, felt their touches, so he kept them safe.

They did find his huge shaft hanging above them. Kim's eyes widened and she grabbed it with both hands. The dinosaur was able to bend his neck to the side and watch as Kim massaged his shaft, and Erin sucked on Kim's boobs and fingered her.

"I think he's about to come," Kim said excitedly and the dinosaur groaned.

Erin joined her and they both stroked his large shaft together until it throbbed and he spluttered his thick fluids all over their bodies.

The ladies screamed delightfully and turned to each other, looking at the fluids dripping down their bodies. They kissed and smeared each other with the stuff, feeling the hotness of the moment. With their hands between each other's legs, fingering each other until they shuddered and screamed out, climaxing together.

Kim and Erin spent the rest of their time with the supersaurus, riding on its back, feeling the cold night air on their bodies, making out right on top of its body. They explored the dinosaur's body, grinding sexually and pleasuring the magnificent creature in ways it had never felt before.

**

It was finally time to return back to their timeline and Kim was a little downcast by the idea. She'd had more fun than she'd ever had before, and was still struck by the awe of interacting sexually with a prehistoric creature—and also the sexiness and intensity of doing so with Erin as a partner.

"I know the feeling," Erin said. She put her arms around Kim and pulled her in for a soft kiss. "But at least, you've got me."

"Yeah, but what if things between us aren't as exciting as it is now? I had so much fun with you here because we both shared this amazing connection with a creature lost in time. What if it's all dampened by, you know, the boring real world?"

Erin thought about this for a while. She understood Kim's fears, and it had also occurred to her. She also knew how she felt each time she had to travel back to the future after a hot, sexy adventure.

"You know what," she said, grinning. "If it gets boring, we could always travel back in time for another adventure. It's just like I always did…well, before I got banned."

Kim's eyes widened. "That's right. If it gets dull, we can always spice things up with some prehistoric sexual adventure!"

They both activated their time belts, happy to be with each other and excited about the prospects of a future dinosaur tryst, despite still having a trace of doubt lingering in the back of their heads.

Bonus:

Tyrannosaurus Sext

This is ridiculous, and Alice knows it.

There's no good reason for her to be here right now, at 8 PM on a Tuesday evening, standing outside the high cement fence that surrounds the headquarters of Hi-Tec Inc. There is, however, a bad reason - or at least a potentially ill-advised one.

His name is Rex.

She's here because for the last three weeks, she's been talking to Rex online, and this is where they're supposed to meet. She always promised herself she'd never use dating apps. But she'd broken up with her ex months ago after five years together, and as she became increasingly frustrated, she figured it couldn't hurt to try, right? And Rex seemed nice. He said the right things. He seemed to have similar… preferences. The sexting was fun. How bad could he be?

But Alice is starting to have suspicions. He's twenty minutes late. *At least this place has got to have security cams in case something happens,* she thinks. *They sell them.*

She hugs her arms around her chest, burrowing into her heavy jacket. It's late autumn and she can see her breath in the glow of the floodlight. She wishes she had someone to keep her warm.

Suddenly, there's a thump.

It's a heavy sound, like something being dropped. Alice startles, and then there's another. Thump. Thump. Thump. It's a rhythm, she realizes. It's *footsteps.* The footsteps of something absolutely massive. She holds her breath.

It's not terribly uncommon for corporations like this to employ dinosaurs as their security guards. They aren't usually suitable for more intellectual pursuits, and they're excellent thief-deterrents. The Revival happened when Alice was small, and she's no stranger to the sight of a dino, but it's been rare for her to see one up close.

Even if she's being stood up, it'll be nice to gawk at a beast.

Alice is a little worried that she'll get in trouble for loitering, but she stands her ground. She wants to stay in range of the security cams. And she's not doing anything so terrible, right? Just a girl, standing by a wall, being stood up by a date. Happens thousands of times a day.

And then the dinosaur peeks over the top of the cement wall. It's a tyrannosaurus rex, wearing a security guard uniform. "Alice?"

The voice is a deep rumbling, almost a purr. It's smooth and rough all at once. Alice stares with wide eyes. "How did you know my name?"

“Alice… as in… Alice Palace Ninety Five?” the tyrannosaurus rex asks.

“Oh my God,” says Alice. “Are you – are you King Of The City?”

That’s Rex’s screen name.

Their conversations started out as something else, something more gentle. They had just been talking about everyday things at first, the basic getting-to-know-you chatter that confirms that this is a person worth talking to. They had hit it off so well that things had gone further than she expected them to. And it had been *fun*.

King Of The City had been great at it. He had told her things that had brought Alice straight to the edge, her fingers working over her pussy as she read about all the things that he would do to her.

If only he could.

So they had decided to meet up here, so that he could.

Alice had assumed that King of the City, whomever he was, worked here. Maybe he'd been nervous, like her, and had wanted to be in full view of the security cameras. But it had never once crossed her mind that the man would be a *dinosaur.*

She hadn't known that they were capable of such intellectual banter, or such thrilling wordplay. She certainly hadn't known that they were interested in sex with humans. But here she is, and here he is, and an unexpected thrill rises in her.

Rex tilts his head to the side, so he can get a better look at her. "You're even prettier in person. I didn't think that it would be… like this."

"You're a dinosaur," says Alice.

The dinosaur tilts his head to the side, looking almost ashamed. "I should have said something. Before you came out here, I mean. I understand if you want to leave now."

Alice thinks back to the last message that she had gotten from him. King Of The City had told Alice that he would make her feel like the ultimate queen.

He had gone into great detail about how good he was with his tongue. As he speaks with that rumbly voice of his, she can see flashes of it between his sharp teeth. It's long. It must be dextrous. Prehensile.

She knows that this is something special. That everything Rex had told her is true. She knows he's a rare dinosaur. She knows he wants her. Those teeth flash in the floodlight, adding an almost dangerous edge to the fantasy.

Alice has never been one for danger, but she can feel her tastes shifting and expanding as she takes in the sight of Rex's body: his powerful jaws, keen and flashing eyes. His mouth. Right now, all she wants is for that massive dinosaur head to be buried between her legs, and her thighs to be pressed against either side of his massive, scaly muzzle.

Her cheeks, already ruddy from the cold, go even pinker. She's surprised herself.

Rex says, "I understand that you want to leave. I do. Not a lot of people would be alright with this, and I know that. I'm sorry I didn't tell you sooner."

"It's okay," Alice says. "I'm not leaving."

Rex tilts his head again, clearly surprised. "Are you sure? I don't want to do anything that would make you uncomfortable."

"I want to do the things we talked about all week," says Alice. "I've never been with a dinosaur, but I want to try."

As she speaks, she realizes that it's true. She wants to try new things. Her last relationship had been stifling: her ex had very simple tastes, and was never interested in spicing things up. At the time, she thought it was just how things were. But now there's a dinosaur, a whole *dinosaur*, standing in front of her, beckoning her in. He's enormous and powerful and intelligent. This is exactly what she needs.

"Follow me," says Rex. He walks along the wall, tall enough that it's easy for her to follow along, and leads Alice to a metal gate at the far side of the building. He opens it for her and it rises with a whirr. She steps inside.

Rex is even bigger once he's in full view. And though Alice knows that it's a strange thing to think, she also can't deny the fact that he's terribly handsome. There's a sheen to his skin, a green and mottled shading that draws the eye.

His golden eyes are huge and vaguely catlike, and his mouth is filled with rows of massive sharp teeth. He hunkers down, using his fingers to tap at the keypad. The gate closes behind them. Rex says, "it took me a long time to figure out how to do this. But I've gotten pretty good."

"I'd say you're pretty good," says Alice. "You're very good. I look forward to seeing just how good you are." She can't quite believe she's being so forward.

Rex towers above her. Slowly, Alice reaches out and puts a hand on the curve of his belly. His skin is smooth and ridged beneath her palm. She's surprised, somehow: she thought he would be clammy and cold, but he's warm, and his skin is yielding. She rubs at him for a moment, and then tilts her head back and smiles.

She asks him, "Do you work here?"

"I live here," he says, leading the way into the facility grounds. His tail doesn't drag against the ground but rather sways as a counterbalance to his bulk, and it's easy to follow along. His steps are large but slow. "Are you sure you're okay with this?"

"I came out here because I liked you. I liked talking to you," says Alice, honestly.

Rex leads her to a section of the

grounds that has clearly been converted for dinosaur living. Rather than stairs leading up into apartments, there are stairs that lead down into an underground complex with high ceilings, hewn into the clay. It's surprisingly homey, lit with fairy lights strung up across the walls. "There are a few of us who live here," Rex says, "but the others are elsewhere. It's just us right now. We'll have privacy."

He leads Alice into an apartment just off the main communal space. It's decorated modestly but tastefully, mostly with low-light plants. A little water fountain in the corner gurgles serenely.

There's a large circular couch-like structure with a dip in the back for Rex's tail to hang over the side of it.

Alice looks around. "I like it."

"You like it."

"I do," says Alice. She unzips the front of her jacket and throws it over the back of the couch. She's wearing a pair of tight jeans and a low-cut blouse. Rex openly stares at her cleavage. His cock is already starting to protrude from his vent.

It's thick.

Even barely visible, she can tell that. The head of his cock is tapered and it's a brilliant sort of flushed red. Thick as four fingers right at the top, and then thicker still as it slides down.

Alice always knew that she would be getting a little bit tonight. It just turns out that she's going to be getting a *lot* instead.

She thinks about how Rex had texted her about wanting to undress her slowly, how his messages had taken great care to explain that. So she gives him what he wanted. She slowly pulls off her blouse and tosses it onto the floor, and then reaches down to unhook the front of her jeans. She slides those down as well, revealing the fact that she isn't wearing any panties beneath. Rex reaches his huge head down to help, hooking a tooth into one of the belt loops and pulling them off of her.

Once her clothes are on the floor, she steps forward, and she takes hold of the dinosaur's cock. It takes both hands to wrap fully around it, rubbing over the length. As she touches Rex, his cock continues to grow in size.

It's absolutely massive. Thick around as a soda can and just as long as her forearm, with a ribbed texture to it that makes her mouth start to water. She'd never imagined that she would be *attracted* to a dinosaur, but in this moment, she can't imagine how she'd ever lived without this.

Rex makes a crooning sound in the back of his throat, sitting down a little bit so it's easier for Alice to reach. She works over the length of his cock with both hands, gathering up the copious amounts of pre cum that he's spilling and using it to help slick the way.

"Easy," she croons back at him.

Rex's breath catches, and then with a rumble, he says, "We don't have to. If this is too… off putting for you."

Alice says, "Do I look like I'm unhappy?" She smiles up at him. "I wouldn't be here if I didn't want to be. I want this. I want you."

With that settled, she turns back to focusing fully on Rex, on trying to make him as comfortable as she can. And if he's being honest, it's pretty hot, getting to jack off someone that's so much larger than she is.

The thought of actually being *fucked* with that thing? Oh, that gets Alice really hot and bothered and very wet between the legs. She swipes her thumbs against the underside of the dinosaur's flared cock head, and then drags them down, down over a thick vein in the side.

Rex is leaking more now, his cock pulsing between her hands. She can tell that he's close. The dinosaur is breathing hard, huffing out through his flaring nostrils, growling with pleasure as he rolls his hips, juddering them against her hands.

And then he's coming, thick ropes of it spilling over Alice's hands. It's hot, and thicker than a man's cum. And there's just so much of it that it seems to be everywhere at once, too much to hold. If he had come inside of her, it would surely make her belly bloat up with the force of it.

Her eyes flutter, just thinking about this massive cock being inside of her enough to get her practically dripping in her panties.

She pulls back, looking up at him from under her eyelashes. "Wow. You, uh, you're even better than the messages made you seem. But…" She takes a step backwards, moving to sit on the edge of the circular couch and spreading her legs, letting one hand settle between them. "I think it's my turn now, don't you?"

"Yeah," says Rex. "I really, really do."

ABOUT THE AUTHOR

From an early age Lola Faust's fantasies and reveries tilted towards the baroque, the unusual, and the eccentric. Though she entertained curious private journals, it wasn't until she entered the Paleontology program at the University of British Columbia that her fantastic and romantic notions concerning dinosaurs took full flight.

While working towards her doctorate, Ms Faust began writing her signature saurian prose. Today she is employed by day at a leading university in her field, but maintains her anonymous and risque personality online.